ALCHEMY

The Night of a Thousand Desires. A Premiered Collection of Adults Stories to Enjoy Your Lockdown Time

Mia Abbey

TABLE OF CONTENTS

THE SWAP

Jim and Karen lived a few doors away from their best friends Peter and Wendy. All were in their mid-thirties and had known each other since college and had spent many holidays and social events together since then.

One Friday night, they found themselves in a group of eight at a wine tasting with several neighbors from the immediate area.

The wine had loosened a few tongues, and some of the questions became quite personal.

"You four are out with other people, that makes a change," came a comment referring to Jim, Karen, Peter and Wendy.

"We mix in larger groups, go out as a couple, as individuals, but as a group of four we have many common interests," Karen explained.

"Is one of those common interests a bit of bartering?" asked Matt, who talked about a bottle of wine over his limit and a big mouth at the best of times.

The group groaned in embarrassment, although secretly many would have liked to know the truth.

"There was nothing to report, no exchange of any kind," Peter offered.

All this had put a damper on the party and our four left early and went to Jim and Karen.

Jim put a bottle of wine and four glasses on the coffee table.

"We've all had enough wine, but just in case..."

They were all quiet for a while because the wine tasting had been disappointing.

"We gave them more ammunition when we left, now they imagine us all naked and lying in a heap on the carpet," Wendy remarked.

"You cannot control what other people imagine," said Peter.

"I can't blame them, I know what I would think if I were outside the group," Jim said.

"Are we all as pure as the driven snow, does anyone here want to confess that they have thoughts about another person in the group?

They were quiet for a while, then Karen spoke up.

"Remember that holiday in Scotland, it was Edinburgh, an Indian and a Chinese restaurant had been recommended, but we couldn't agree on where to eat. I took Peter and Jim to Chinese, and Wendy went to Indian.

"I reached for the soy sauce and rubbed my arm against Peter's arm, I held his arm and slowly pulled him away. That set me on fire, I think if we hadn't agreed to regroup later, I might have apologised by taking off my panties.

That was a wild thing to do by group standards. Not to be outdone was Wendy had a story to tell.

"We were on this cruise in the Mediterranean, and I hurt my foot. It was splinted in hospital, which made walking in the old cities quite a challenge. The three of them kept holding a hand or an elbow to give me support. I loved holding hands with Jim, I wore the splint and bandages longer than necessary.

Peter was next: "My weakness is to mentally undress Karen. In the unlikely event that I ever see her breasts or pussy, I wonder if they will look the way I imagine them to.

"That's no secret," Wendy said, "I often wonder if your intense looks will set her clothes on fire.

"That just leaves me," said Jim, "I keep dreaming of being shipwrecked with Wendy on a small tropical island. We never get over the problem of sand in our genitals."

"We are not quite as tense as we thought," commented Wendy.

The girls seem to like holding hands, it sounds very innocent, will someone change places?" Peter asked.

Peter and Karen made themselves comfortable on one two-seater, Jim and Wendy on the other.

They came closer and felt the warmth of their partner's thighs, held hands and talked quietly.

Peter and Karen's lips came closer and closer as they whispered. Jim and Wendy did the same. Each couple watched the other's progress. When the kissing began, there were no objections.

Karen climbed onto Peter's lap. Wendy immediately followed with Jim.

Karen opened her blouse: "You wanted to see if my breasts were the same as they appear in my dreams?

Peter reached for her and let go of her bra.

"In my dreams they were perfect, and they're even better in real life."

Jim was now kneeling on the floor in front of Wendy on the sofa with one hand on each thigh under her skirt, sucking on her nipples.

No one else dared to go on that evening, they ended the evening as if nothing extraordinary had happened, and Peter and Wendy set off for home.

They did not meet again until Sunday afternoon, when they went for a walk in the country and ended up at Peter and Wendy's house.

It was obvious that they needed a debriefing and a plan for the future, but they were all unusually reserved.

Jim broke the ice: "That was a great evening, my heart rate still hasn't normalized. Can I assume that we will all stay with our current loving spouses, with the possibility of further 'exchange' initiatives?

"Well said," Peter said.

The ladies both nodded in agreement and looked very pleased with themselves.

Peter and Jim decided to watch the rest of a game on TV, the ladies went into the kitchen to heat up some snacks and put on the coffee.

The game was over, the smell of coffee and food poured in from the kitchen.

Peter and Jim sat relaxed in their chairs, completely unprepared for their next surprise.

The ladies each came in with a tray of food and coffee - they only wore bras and panties.

"Remind me to tip the waitresses, Peter, lovely young girls," Jim asked.

"Peter has seen me naked on his bucket list, he's seen my breasts tonight, he might see my pussy. Karen explained.

"I suppose Jim and I will keep up with you - or go ahead," laughed Wendy.

Jim and Peter carried the trays back into the kitchen and put the dishes in the dishwasher.

When they returned to the family room they were presented with a wonderful sight. The ladies were naked and practicing dance steps to background music.

They asked the boys to sit down.

"Undress before you make yourself comfortable," Wendy demanded.

"Sorry, we're hopeless at dancing to stripper music and totally incompetent at lap dancing, but we'll do what we can," Karen explained.

"That's great, don't apologize," said Peter on behalf of the male audience.

Karen stood up on Peter's chair, lap dancing style, with one foot on each side of his thighs. That brought her pussy up to his face level.

"As beautiful as in your dreams?" she asked.

"Perfect." was all Peter could say.

"I wanted to split the lips of my pussy to show all my wealth, but I have to keep my balance, would you assist me, please?

Peter gently parted her pussy lips with his thumb and forefinger.

"I only have a tiny clitoris, maybe you can make it grow with your tongue," she invited.

Peter reached both hands, spread her pussy lips and tried to bury his face.

Jim and Wendy were at the same stage on the adjacent sofa.

The ladies changed their position and sat down on the boys' laps to kiss and touch each other.

"We can't leave you with angry erections," Wendy said, "I'll look for tissues and oils or lotions and hope that handwork is enough for the grand finale tonight.

Wendy instructed Jim to lie on his back on the floor and she overcame him in the style of 69, giving him a short lollipop before applying oil generously. He stuck one finger of one hand into her pussy and grabbed a breast with the other hand.

Karen had Peter on her hands and knees. She stood under him and turned down to suck his cock. Then she moved and positioned her breasts under his cock. Partly hand-fucked and partly tit-fucked, he made a deposit between her tits. Karen rubbed him against her skin and licked her fingers clean.

Jim and Karen went home, past the four neighbours who were also at the last party. They were standing in front of one of their houses, each with a glass of wine in his hand.

There were exchanged pleasantries, Jim and Karen felt suspicious.

"If they only knew what we've been up to lately," Karen laughed.

Within the group of four, nothing was said or discussed about the following weekend, except that they were to have lunch at a fish restaurant, followed by coffee and cake at Jim and Karen's place.

Maybe coffee and cake is a euphemism for coffee, cake, oral and vaginal sex?

In the middle of the afternoon Jim and Peter were in Jim's workshop when the ladies called them into the house. Wendy took Jim's hand; Karen took Peter and they went upstairs to the second and third bedrooms.

Wendy and Jim undressed quickly, he put his arms around her, grabbed her bottom and was up and in her before she reached the mattress. It lasted less than a minute.

"She laughed, "You have to catch the bus?

"Without that I would have been bursting at the seams, now I'll do anything you want, at your service.

"I'll finish off with a back and front massage with two fingers in the pussy and French kissing, then I'll ride you cowgirl. After that we will cuddle and sleep until we are hungry enough to go downstairs at six or seven.

Peter and Karen had a different approach. They kissed and cuddled on the bed before they undressed.

"Karen asked: 'Kiss and lick me from top to toe with special attention to my tits and pussy. If you do a good job, I'll do something similar to you. Then we'll decide whether we'll fuck first and then take a nap or take the nap first and then fuck before we go down for dinner.

That night, everyone agreed that they were anxious to fuck their spouses when they returned to their own beds, but they admitted they would fall asleep before anything happened.

SWIMMING AND SWAPPING

Angus and Sophia had been in their house for fifteen years. Angus was an avid do-it-yourselfer, and since Sophia was busy with the design and gardens, they had the house in good condition.

Their new neighbor's Bruno and Amelia were younger and they had bought a house at a bargain price that had not changed much since the 1970s. They worked hard to catch up with the furniture and improve their skills.

Many conversations took place over the fence, especially on weekends.

On one Saturday the residents on both sides of the fence were very busy until they stopped at about 5 pm.

Angus' last words were: "Skinny dipping our pool 8 pm sharp".

"You and your big mouth and your strange sense of humor, they may never speak to us again," Sophia lamented.

"Whenever we use our pool, it's usually just after dusk because you like the lights - and we go in naked so we don't have to rinse our bathers or destroy them with the chlorine.

"Yes, but we have no company and we invite them to be naked."

"A quick look at Amelia's tits would be better than a five-star movie."

"They're probably no prettier than mine."

"Probably not, but variety is the spice of life, and it could be detail, firmness, nipple length, colouring or something interesting.

"Angus, I think you're getting worse as you get older.

Around 8pm, Angus and Sophia were swimming naked in their pool and thought it highly unlikely they'd have company - until Bruno and Amelia walked in and had nothing on unless you count the two curled up towels Bruno was wearing

The visitors ran wildly towards the pool, shouting 'Good evening' as they bombed into the water.

"Do you often have lean dip evenings here," Amelia asked.

"Just us, never in company before, I thought Angus might have offended you, what about you, are you regulars in the nude bathing scene?

"Twice before, when we went to a mixed onsen in Japan, Bruno was disappointed because the ladies had such small tits, even if they were more to his taste, he couldn't have seen them through the steam.

"Another time, we jumped into a pond beside Ben Nevis in Scotland. Although it was the middle of summer, it was so cold that we couldn't find Bruno's penis or my nipples for an age afterwards.

"I have to thank you both for lending me tools, recommending craftsmen and advising me on do-it-yourself," said Amelia.

"Why change the subject, I enjoyed the tits and the nude swimming," Angus said, getting a serious look from Sophia.

They stayed in the water for an hour and Sophia suggested they have coffee on the terrace.

"You both reflect us in some way, the men have a strange sense of humour and we are all quite frank," commented Sophia.

"You can't argue with that," said Amelia, "it feels as if we've known you for years.

"You both, how shall I put it, come over here naked in response to something that could have been a joke, that's very daring, lead an exciting social life,"

Angus asked.

"Do we get along with other people, is that what you want to say?" asked Bruno.

"That's none of our business, we're just talking," Angus replied, sounding apologetic.

"We have swum naked with other people, two, now three times. Twice we've been to parties that were about gentle swapping. We didn't go back to reach higher levels of swapping.

"I'm curious, what exactly is soft-swapping?"

Partners are swapped to kiss. Normally, on this level, everyone is in the same room. Depending on the group, the rules may allow touching above the waist, under or over the clothes".

"Sounds like harmless fun," Angus said, "I'm ready when the rest of you are ready too.

"I think we must discuss this Angus," Sophia said sternly.

"We've just done that. All those in favour, raise your hand."

Three and a half votes in favor, counting a somewhat weak arm rising from Sophia.

The girls went into the house to freshen up and came back in underpants.

"Topless smooching, here we come," said an excited Bruno.

They started with the men sitting on patio chairs, with one girl on each lap. For greater comfort, they went on couches and lay down horizontally.

Within thirty minutes, they all emerged to get some air. After a very exhausting day they were tired and waking up on a cramped couch would not lead to a productive Sunday.

Amelia asked Sophia how she was feeling.

"I've always been a bit of a prude. A few hours ago I would have divorced Angus because he agreed to a gentle swing, he almost got kicked out because he invited you to swim naked. My attitude changes from minute to minute.

"It has to do with the feeling that we have known you for years and like and respect you both so much that the whole process is accelerated and exciting.

"Now I wonder what would give me more pleasure, a good hard fuck with Bruno or watching Angus fuck Amelia - but not tonight, I'm knackered."

"Well, same time, same place, same order of undress, tomorrow?" Bruno asked.

"Will I see you for coffee sometime during the day to plan the evening?" Angus suggested.

There was a lot of excitement in the air the following day at the morning coffee.

"Shall we swap places after our swim tonight?" Bruno asked.

"Shall we all continue with kissing and touching above the waist? asked Angus.

Four hands were raised very quickly.

"That's the tricky part, do we add oral sex on women, blowjobs, vaginal sex as a gradual process or do we jump ahead with our feet.

"All this," they shouted in unison.

Do we really have to develop a set of rules or do we just have to play it by ear? asked Sophia.

"Rule number one for most groups should be No means no. But I cannot imagine that there are insoluble border issues within this group," Amelia noted.

"In some groups, there might be jealousy because a couple only kiss and their spouses are kissing each other, and their spouses are going at it over the top full-gender. That wouldn't apply to us either," said Sophia.

"You know, these deck chairs are not meant for two. Shouldn't the ladies go into the comfort of their own bed and let the men change the house, or is that too bold at the moment? asked Angus.

"I would feel very safe in this situation with my spouse next door. And Sophia, if my husband tries to enter the wrong hole and doesn't take no for an answer, you have my permission to cut his balls off with a plastic spoon. exclaimed Amelia.

"Just kidding, Bruno, I know you'll treat Sophia with the same kindness and respect I get." She went on.

The swimming lesson went on as before, only this time Bruno and Amelia bombed the water and shouted: Rubba Dubba Doo!

The coffee on the terrace was drunk very quickly. Angus and Amelia went next door, Bruno and Sophia went upstairs.

Bruno and Sophia hopped into bed.

Sophia called her husband: "I'm about to pick up another man's cock, the first time since I met you. I love you," said Sophia.

He replied, "We're off to a slow start, but tonight my cock goes in Amelia's mouth and pussy, the first time since we met, it's somewhere else than with you. I love you, sweet dreams."

He hung up the phone and reached for the pussy.

"Oral sex in both directions, me on top, then lots of cuddling and a good night's sleep," Sophia asked.

"Sounds perfect," he replied, "Let me know if you're not feeling well or if you want me to do something special, can't wait to find the most sensitive parts of your pussy lips.

Next door, Angus and Amelia collapsed in armchairs, each with a glass of iced water, to get some rest before the main event. They recovered quickly,

Amelia approached him on her knees with a mouth full of ice. She took his cock in her mouth and used her tongue and swirled the ice and her tongue with great effect.

When enough ice had melted so that she could speak, she said, "I think if this was done properly, it would be alternately hot and cold.

How was that?"

"Incredibly good", and with that he moved her back to her chair and slowly fed ice cubes into her vagina with his tongue.

"How was that?"

"More than amazing."

So, they went upstairs and had Angus-on-top missionary sex and snuggled up until morning

The next day was a holiday. They all sat around the morning coffee cups and looked, as they say, like cats that had been in the cream.

They agreed to schedule an extra night once a month for their birthdays, holidays, National Windbag Day, St. Patrick's Day, King Solomon's birthday and any other special events that might arise.

THE NEW FRIENDS

My wife Mary and I met some new friends last Friday evening in a café in the city central when things took an interesting turn.

To describe Mary first, she has 5'6 long, taut legs, big 40D breasts that have just begun to yield to gravity, a round, firm ass and only a hint of a belly. She has long dark brown hair and beautiful deep brown eyes that give a hint of Indian descent. I am 1.90 m tall, have a shaved head to hide the quick baldness, broad shoulders, a somewhat thick belly, but overall a stature that is above average for a man.

We had been talking online with Ken and Kathy for a few weeks, we had met in a swinger's group and talked about movies and general nerdy stuff. This was to be our first meeting face to face, and a café seemed ideal. It is a neutral territory. Nobody feels pressured when they are near a private room, nobody is forced by alcohol to make decisions they might regret later.

When Ken and Kathy came in, I was devastated. We had of course exchanged pictures, even some naughty ones, but the camera didn't do them justice. Ken looked like a male model, like the hero on action figure packages. He was bald, full lips, dark eyes and a natural smile. His shirt bulged and rippled when he moved his arms, his muscles contracted and threatened to burst at any moment. Kathy looked like an Amazon. She was six feet tall, slim, dark night-black, with cheeky breasts, wide hips and long legs, accentuated by a miniskirt that constantly revealed her amazing ass.

I stood up and shook Ken's hand as they approached and gave Kathy a light one-armed hug. We talked for a moment, and then Ken and I went to the counter to order while the wives got to know each other a little. What attracted us to each other at first were movies, and it wasn't long before Ken and I talked at length about the new movies that were coming out, and what movies we thought were hot garbage, and which ones looked so bad they were good. While we waited for our drinks, I took a look back at the table and looked up Kathy's skirt for a moment, not sure if it was on purpose or not. I told Ken that Kathy looked amazing and he replied that Mary was an absolute knockout, an opinion I agreed with, but it was nice to hear others say that.

After a few hours of sitting and talking and three cups of coffee later, we decided to move this conversation to my and Kathy's house to play some board games and get to know each other over drinks.

As we both had a drink at the dining table, we started handing out cards for a few rounds of Cards against Humanity. It was a great icebreaker game full of inappropriate laughter. I kept staring at Kathy and noticed that Ken and Mary were also appreciating each other. After a few drinks and a few rounds we started to play a strip version. Whose card was chosen as the winner was allowed to choose one of the other players to remove an item of clothing. It didn't take long before we had Mary and Kathy stripped down to their bras and panties. Mary was wearing a matching black lace bra with lace-trimmed boys' panties, and Kathie was wearing a red bra and matching thong. Ken and I had both been stripped down to our boxers.

Mary won the round, and as she looked around the table, she finally said: "I just have to see what Kathy's nice tits look like to make the top girl burst! That made us all laugh as Kathy pulled up her bra and let her breasts out. They were smaller than Mary's and perkier, with dark nipple areas on her midnight skin and big nipples. Ken's victory made Mary lose her bra next, Kathy reached behind Mary and unzipped the bra that Mary threw over her head onto the pile of discarded clothes behind her. Her breasts sagged a little, but her fullness and voluptuous nipples still held her full attention.

Kathy won the next round and Mary lost her panties. My wife got up from her seat and stepped onto the table, taking care not to disturb the cards or the drinks, and slowly rolled her panties down her legs, spinning in a slow circle as she bent down and pushed it up to her ankles, she bent down lower and exposed both Ken and Kathy's ass and pussy, she turned her head over her shoulder to Kathy, "is this what you wanted to see?

"Is this what you wanted to see?" "You're damn right it is! The pussy's wet enough to lick stamps!" Kathy replied. Mary stood up and stepped out of her panties and left it in the middle of the table before stepping back. Kathy helped her down and ran her hand up Mary's inner thigh as she stepped back.

"Well, I guess I'm out of the game now, so I get to watch," Mary said as she sat down on the chair with her legs slightly spread.

This time I won, and I looked between the two new friends we'd made: "I can't wait to see Kathy's delicious pussy, but I think if Ken stays in these boxers any longer, his boner will come out of them and tear them apart, so let Ken see what you've got! This surprised everyone a little bit, but only for a moment before Ken started giggling and stood up and peeled off his boxer shorts and revealed a massive cock that was as coconut brown as the rest of him. It hung long and the stuff between his legs was a light ten inches and a good three inches in diameter. It was the second largest tail I had ever seen, and the largest was a soccer player we all hated to shower with in high school because there was simply no comparison. Ken pushed back his chair and occasionally stroked his cock to get it to full erection while Kathy and I finished the last round.

We decided that the only fair way to do this was to give Mary the opportunity to choose the winning card. This time it was Kathy who climbed onto the table and unfastened the strings on the side of her thong that was holding her, as

she climbed back down, Mary stood up and grabbed it. Kathy sat down on the table and Mary kissed her. I could see their tongues flirting into and out of each other's mouths.

Mary broke the kiss and lightly pressed on Kathy's shoulder to signal that she should sit back, which she did. Mary then began to kiss her breasts and licked the left nipple first, then the right. She moved her kisses onto Kathy's flat stomach and onto her hips. Mary kissed and then bit slightly on the skin of Kathy's inner thigh. Kathy arched her hips slightly upwards and Mary moved her mouth closer to Kathy's pussy lips. She teasingly licked her clitoris with the tip of her tongue. As I watched my wife lick Kathy's cunt, I pushed my boxers down and freed my hardened cock.

My cock is thicker than average, but only slightly, depending on my horniness and the weather it is between 6 and 8 centimeter's, it is quite thick, but the best part of my cock is the head. It has the circumference of a tennis ball, most of the women I have been with have no problem taking my full length, but my full circumference is another story. Mary herself had trouble with it until after our second child. Now I watched her sucking and licking this other woman's sweet-smelling pussy and I started to caress myself lightly.

Kathy moaned and pulled Mary's face deeper into her spread legs and lifted her hips as she orgasmed, only to finally calm down again. Mary sat up and then climbed over Kathy's body onto the table, curled up and kissed a new way up her body until she reached her face, kissing her deeply and passionately before turning around and lowering her own soaking wet cunt onto Kathy's eager mouth before diving back hungrily for more of Kathy's sperm. Kathy pushed her tongue inside my wife, licked the outer folds of her lips and then sucked on her clitoris.

As I rubbed my hard cock, I felt a hand gently caress my balls. I looked down and saw Ken massaging my balls, he looked at me and smiled, now I have never been with another man, I have never found any man sexually attractive. I've seen guys that look good, but they didn't do anything for me, but that was sending a little bit of electricity through my loins that became a full power plant when Ken bent down and started sucking just the head of my cock. He licked and sucked the head and let it jump out of his mouth with an audible pop every now and then. I leaned back the head and closed my eyes as he teased my cock. I had never kissed another man before, let alone had a duck on my cock, it was a strange feeling. I felt the stubble of his bread rubbing against my balls and thighs and tickling as he maneuvered my cock around in his mouth. He was talented at it, he kept bringing me to the brink of orgasm and then pulling me back again.

Kathy and Mary both orgasm together on the table, and Ken kept bringing me to the brink of orgasm before pulling back and letting me calm down. As the women came towards us, Ken stood up and kissed Mary on the mouth while Kathy fell on my lap and wrapped her arms and legs around me.

My cock found her dripping wet appearance easy and she started rocking her hips and pushing me deeper inside. Her pussy snuggled around my cock and stroked my length from the inside. I bent down and licked her nipple, took one in my mouth and bit her slightly. "Mmmmm", she moaned "harder!" I bit harder on her nipple and rolled it between my teeth. She bucked and pressed hard on my lap and I felt her sperm roll past my balls.

Over Kathy's shoulder I could see Mary bending over the table and Ken ramming his cock into her. She gasped for breath and moaned violently as he hammered into her, her hands gripping the sides of the table. She opened her eyes and watched as Kathy twitched in my lap before another orgasm. I grabbed Kathy's shoulders and began to push her body down while I pushed my hips up and penetrated deeper into her until I finally cramped my cock in her pussy and filled her with my sperm. Kathy moaned as I shot my load into her, then she leaned in and gasped for air, kissed me on the lips and then on the neck. She rose from me, small drops of our cum dripping freely and she made her way back to the table and climbed to the top in front of Mary. She spread her legs and pulled Mary's face into her neatly trimmed pussy. "Fuck you clean!" She moaned, "Lick your husband's sperm off my pussy."

That was all Mary needed when she drove her face in and wrapped an arm around Kathy's leg to hold her down. Ken grabbed Mary's hips and punched harder, obviously turned on by the show that was going on in front of him, until finally I saw his leg start to twitch and he cried out a deep throaty moan, and I knew he had just reached orgasm and was emptying his balls into my wife. Mary collapsed on top of Kathy, and Ken staggered back into the chair next to me.

This was the first time the four of us played together, but I hoped it wouldn't be the last.

THE SUMMER DAY

There is nothing more beautiful than a wonderful summer day in the cities. It was a Friday afternoon, and I was having a few beers with some friends in a bar by a lake. We are all teachers at a local high school and take full advantage of an afternoon without work. Joni is teaching social studies right next to me. Matt, who is also Joni's husband, is an English teacher at the other end of the building. Joni and Matt are a few years younger than my 31 years, and they are good friends with my wife, Kate and me. Kate is not a teacher, so she gets a bit jealous of our seasonal freedom.

We had a few pitchers of beer when Matt asked if Kate would join us later.

"I think so. She gets off work at 4:00 today, so she'll be down in about half an hour. Can we have dinner later?"

"I think we probably should," Joni replied, "This is the first chance we've had to hang out with you guys this summer. With all the time we spent in the cabin, we weren't sociable enough, and we'd love to spend more time with you guys.

She winked at me when she said that, which I found a little weird, but Joni has always been a little weird. Both she and Matt started working at the same school as me two years ago. We were friends, but it wasn't until this year that we became close friends. Joni was the teacher the kids loved. She was a hip young role model for the girls and a physical role model for the hormone-driven boys. I certainly didn't mind that a petite, strapping blonde worked 25 meters away from me. It kept my mind from wandering to the tits the teenage girls at school were so proud of and showing off with.

Matt doesn't mind that Joni is the object of so many teenage fantasies, and in fact, some girls (and a few boys) have a big crush on him. His fit physique, brown hair and eyes and short beard look strong, but he has a cool, literature-loving attitude.

After further conversations about how our summer had gone and about the students we keep coming back to, Kate showed up smiling. She was wearing a blue sundress that showed off her long athletic legs. Joni stood up to hug her and the contrast in her heights was dramatic. Katie had to bend her 1.5-foot frame down to meet Joni's 1.5-foot frame. It was a beautiful sight for Matt and me when Joni's short white skirt blew in the wind and standing on her toes strained her slender legs and tight butt. My wife leaned over and showed a bit more cleavage than she probably knew, and Joni gave her a quick hickey on the lips. When my wife was surprised, she didn't show it.

We sat together for an hour or two and talked, went to dinner and had a really great afternoon with great friends. "What are you gonna do now?" Matt asked. "I'd like to go home and let the dog out, but I don't want the evening to end. Would you like to join us for wine and let the evening continue?"

"That sounds great, but we live in the opposite direction and if I have more wine I might have to attack Dave here," my wife replied smiling and stroked my thigh.

"Joni gets the same when she's drinking. I'm surprised she hasn't fucked someone on the toilet today."

"How do you know I haven't?" she replied with a big grin. "Plus, we have this extra bedroom for both of your problems. If it's too late to go home, just stay the night with us."

Her conversation about Joni screwing someone else was a surprise, even if it was just a joke, but it turned her on a bit. We agreed to have a drink with them and we all got in a taxi. I sat in the front to accommodate my 6 foot 2-inch-wide shouldered frame, and the other three piled in the back. I could see Joni leaning into my wife more than she needed to. She sat in the middle as the smallest of the group and whispered something to Kate while Matt stroked his wife's leg.

We came to their place, and Matt immediately took out a few bottles of cabernet. Joni put on some music. While they did this, I used the privacy to tell my wife how sexy she looked today.

"Thank you very much. You look pretty sexy yourself, and it seems that Joni would agree with that. On the way here, she told me how she said she could attack you here too and that she was jealous that I would get fucked by it.

"She said this while sitting right next to Matt!?" I asked incredulously.

"I think he heard it and seemed turned on by it. She should also be a bit jealous, you're hot. Not that I'm not a bit jealous of her, Matt is a sexy man."

At that point, Joni came back and danced her jazzy beats Matt was right behind her while wine stared at Joni's swaying ass moving in front of him. Matt sat down in the armchair and Joni quickly took the middle of the sofa, leaving the ends free for me and Kate. As we sat and joked and listened to the music, the conversation continued to carry its sexual theme.

"I thought you were going to attack Dave?" Joni reminded Kate that.

"I have to admit I was thinking about that big piece of meat all night. Maybe I'll just drag him to your guest room and fuck him twice!"

"Big piece of meat, huh?" and Joni bent over and grabbed my crotch! I was definitely half-eased with all the sexual innuendo, not to mention the two sexy women sharing a couch with me. I tensed up, but Matt and Kate just laughed. "This feels really impressive! I'd love to see it. Kate, do you mind if I pull it out and take a look?"

I don't know if I was more shocked by Joni's audacity, Matt and Kate's laughter or simply the fact that my opinion didn't seem to matter. When Joni started unbuttoning my pants, I looked over at Kate and saw just a sexy smile, so I let it go.

"I'd love to see what kind of 'meat' you're packing," Joni said as she pulled my tail out of my pants. She started stroking it a bit so it could grow. "You're right, that's a nice dick!"

Joni stroked me until I was seven inches tall and tried to put her fingers around my thick shaft. While she was doing this I could see Matt's cock moving in his pants and my wife biting her lip with lust in her eyes and both of them watched as Joni slowly moved my cock to a full erection.

Joni broke the silence. "I know you're looking for some yourself," Kate stared, continuing to stroke my full length. "Since I enjoy your husband's, you could probably find something you can enjoy on your other side.

I looked across the room and Matt had pulled his own stand out of his pants and slowly stroked it while he watched his wife fiddle with mine. His cock was impressive, being over six inches tall and almost as thick as mine. He had a head that looked bigger and the veins bulged thickly. He looked at Kate and gestured to her. She went over to him and knelt down where she could inspect Matt's cock and take it in her hand. Since the boundaries had already been crossed, Kate bent down and took it in her mouth. I felt a touch of jealousy when I saw my wife sucking another man but I quickly got over it when Joni fell down and kissed the head of my cock. Her blue eyes looked up at me as she dropped her mouth and swallowed a good four inches. I put my hand through her curly blonde hair and pushed her further down. She gagged a little while she drooled all over my cock and it felt incredible. She tugged at my balls and stuck them further down her throat than Kate ever could. She bounced up and down while she stroked my shaft hard. Joni enthusiastically sucked a cock and it felt incredible.

As I looked over to my wife, I saw Matt looking at me smiling as I watched Kate do her best tricks that I knew so well. Kate sucked a mean cock and was really after Matt's thick stick. I had trouble pulling Joni off my cock but I didn't want to suck my cock too fast.

Joni has responded to this. "We have all night. It would probably be a good thing if you stuck one down my throat. Then you'd last longer if you start fucking me."

"There's nothing wrong with that logic," and I pushed Joni's head back on my dick. I still had no reason to rush, so I pulled her around. I put one leg over my ear and grabbed her smooth thighs. I always manage to delay orgasm when I'm busy eating pussy.

I don't know if she took her panties off when she wanted to turn on the music or if she was without them all evening, but under the flowing white skirt she was completely open. No underwear. No hair. Just a straight, sleek, shiny, wet pussy. While Joni put the head of my cock back in her mouth, I stuck out my tongue to taste her juicy pussy. I licked her slit up and down a few times, but her small frame made it difficult to reach her. I stuck my tongue into her pussy a few times and tried to suck on her clitoris, but our different heights made it uncomfortable. So, I tried what I could reach. I started rubbing her asshole. She took a quick shot and cramped up, but relaxed quickly. Joni seemed to take my licking on her back hole quite enthusiastically as she pushed her ass back towards my face. I licked around and stuck my tongue into her tight ring while she moaned around my cock. Kate is not as into ass play as I am, so I took advantage of the fact that someone is having so much fun. Then I knew my goal for the evening. To stick my dick in this fantastically tight ass.

"MMmmmmmmmmm!!" I was so engrossed in the blow job I was getting and the ass I was eating that I forgot about my wife until I heard her moan. I looked over, and she was sitting on Matt, who dropped on his dick. I felt a hint of jealousy. We had fooled around a bit, but now there was another man fucking my wife.

Joni might have felt it when she turned around and stroked my dick. "God, they look so sexy. See how much pleasure they feel? I can't wait to feel your dick deep inside of me." Joni moved one leg over my lap and looked me in the eyes. She lowered her pussy down to meet the head of my dick. The crown of my rock-hard shaft slowly worked its way in. Her pussy was wet from her juices and my saliva, but it was just smaller than what my cock is used to. We had to pull it out a few times and put it back in again to stretch her tight pussy. Eventually we worked it in so far that Joni closed her eyes and she just sank into my shaft.

Slowly Joni rocked her body back and forth. I grabbed her hips and pushed her body up and down. Her graceful stature made the difference to Kate's tall, slim body. We fucked slowly until I accepted that it was okay for me to fuck my girlfriend. And that her husband was fucking my wife. I think Joni sensed my lightness when she started to really go for it by fucking on my stiff dick. As my confidence in the situation improved, I started to take more control. I turned her around and put Joni on her hands and knees. As I pushed my cock back into her hot pussy, she sank down to her elbows and moaned.

"Fuck me! Fuck me! Fuck me! Fuck! Fuck! Shit! Fuck me with that big dick!"

I pounded her pussy fast and hard. Something about her still wearing a skirt and a top made her even sexier, but I had to get rid of the restriction of the pants around my knees. I withdrew to take off my inhibiting clothes and Joni took the opportunity to do the same. Her petite frame had perfect hand tits and a beautifully curved ass. I groped her tits and licked her nipples, but had to quickly get back into her hot cunt. I turned her back in doggy style and when I plowed a steel cock back into her cunt, she let out a soft moan. "I'll be right there. I "ll be right there. Keep doing that." I felt obligated and I grabbed her hips and slammed them hard. I was on this beautiful level of alcohol, where I was rock hard but got fucked forever. After a few more minutes of hard pounding in Joni's smooth pussy and fingers on her clit she started shaking and screaming.

"Fuuuuuckkkk!! I'm coming! I'm purring!"

I took advantage of her orgasm to distract her, to further my goal of getting up her ass. I took my pussy-juiced finger and pushed it in her back door when she came. I stuck it in up to the second knuckle when her asshole was squeezed around it. When she came down from her orgasm, she slowly kept bouncing back and forth on my dick. She also let her asshole relax a bit and allowed me to finger her tight ass while I continued to fuck slowly.

I looked over at Kate and Matt and saw my wife coming down from her own orgasm. I know her sex, and that was a big one for her. I expected her to turn over asleep at that moment, but other people had other plans. Matt lifted her off his cock but led her back on her knees and grabbed her head. He tried to get her to suck his cock right after he fucked her! Kate had denied me this pleasure in the past, so I started to feel sorry for Matt because he didn't get his nut, but she opened her mouth and went down! My anger that Kate would do this for him and not for me was short-lived because I had two realizations. One is that Kate opens up and I will be able to cross more boundaries. Two, I'm goanna stick my dick up John's ass.

I watched Kate eagerly swallow as much of Matt's cock as she could bob up and down quickly and hard with her head. Matt grabbed her gently by the hair and helped her to speed up her blow job after fucking. He was in heaven when Kate swallowed his cock up and down. I could see he was about to blow, but I had more pressing and selfish concerns. I was still slowly rocking back and forth in Joni's tight pussy. I was still fingering her asshole. I watched as Joni turned her eyes towards her husband's cock as it disappeared and disappeared again in my wife's eager mouth. It definitely turned her on watching them while she was still bouncing back and forth on my stiff cock. As Matt began to buck his hips more enthusiastically into Kate's mouth, Joni started shaking again. Matt let out a deep "Fuuucckckkkk..." as he blew into my wife's waiting mouth and Joni came back on my cock while she watched with intense eyes. When Matt was done and my wife let his cock fall out of her mouth, Joni spoke up.

"Matt, honey. Why don't you run and get the bottle from the nightstand? Everyone came but Dave. I think that big cock deserves a real reward after all the work he's done." Matt started swinging his cock, and Kate grabbed a sheet to keep warm and curled up on the edge of the sofa. I knew what was coming towards me, so I pulled back to turn Joni around and kiss her deep.

"Here you go, buddy! Don't use it all!" said Matt as he came back and handed me the bottle of lubricant. I wondered how he felt so natural as he walked up to another naked guy and was so casual. I thanked him a little too enthusiastically and opened the lid.

I pushed a big teaspoon and started rubbing it up her asshole. I used my finger to push it a little bit into her asshole while she moaned. I squirted a little and rubbed it on my cock while moving my other greased finger further in and out of her asshole. Joni sat on her knees and moaned softly while Kate stared with big eyes. She seemed in awe and fear of Joni as I prepared us both.

"I can't believe you let him fuck you in the ass! I let him try, but I can't relax. Are you sure he "II fit? You've got such a small bottom, and it's..."

"Sooo... big?" Joni jumped in while Kate thought about how to describe the situation correctly. "And hard? And ready to fill my little bottom?" Joni really knew how to build up the anticipation. "I'm sure it will fit. Matt's dick hits my G-spot from this side when we do this. Not often, but a real treat when we do this. I think Dave hits it without too much trouble and hits it hard. I can't wait to get there while he fucks my ass. He just needs to take it slow to get started. You hear that, Dave? I've got a small ass and my tight little asshole needs you to let go of the fat cock real slow."

"Of course." I said as I started pressing my dick head against that sexy little hole. "I wouldn't dream of just sticking it in." I said, even though I wanted to do exactly that. "I'm just goanna loosen the tip a little bit."

My wife slowly lowered herself to her knees so that she could take a closer look. I still don't think she had blinked since she realized what was about to happen. Meanwhile, Matt sat back down on his chair and started rubbing his re-growing cock again. Joni had her eyes closed and took a deep breath. She made some sounds that were half grunting as if she was working on it and half moaning as if she was jumping on it. I played my part in this show by working my shaft into it piece by piece. I dropped some more lubricant where my cock and her ass were connected. Then I grabbed her left hip with one hand while using the right to guide my central appendage. I pulled back a little bit, more lubricant, then I let go a little bit. Kate still sat there like hypnotized and started to move more and more. Obviously she began to feel the excitement in her own loins. After a more torturous slow repetition of this cycle, I was finally about two inches inside Joni's bottom, and Joni's grunting had turned into a moan. So I began to make deeper strokes. I pulled it out almost all the way and then pumped it back in. Still slow but almost full strokes with my cock. I definitely hit the G-spot from behind every time I went deep.

Joni got off clearly and it spread. Usually too tender for a second round, Kate had started rubbing her recently fucked pussy while watching her husband tap her best friend's ass. Matt was fully erect again and had fallen to the floor behind Kate. She had kneeled down to get a good show and her legs were a little spread. Matt grabbed under her ass and started to help her work on her pussy and clitoris. She was almost hypnotized by the show as she let Matt readjust her position like a puppet while she could still watch closely. He pulled her down on her knees and spread her legs and put her in a similar position to Joni where she was right now. Once he had her in that position, he went down and replaced his fingers with his tongue. The room now filled with two groups of moans, the ever louder and softer moaning of Joni and the almost whispering moan of Kate.

"God, who feels so good... keep fucking. You feel so good in my ass! Keep fucking me, and I'm coming."

I didn't need the encouragement, but I took the direction anyway.

"Your ass is so tight! I fucking love it. I'll be there soon."

"Not until I do! It won't be long!"

"I can hold out for a few minutes, but soon I'll explode! Where will I come?"

"I'd like you to come on my face, but after all the hard work you put into my ass, it wouldn't be fair to force you to retreat, so you should just shoot me in the ass.

"Fuck, yeah. I'm goanna fill your ass with so much semen!"

As I kept fucking Joni at this now frantic pace, I could barely hear Matt asking Kate if she wanted him to fuck her again. She nodded slowly and let out her loudest moan yet as Matt came up behind her again.

"Could you... maybe... touch my bottom?"

I heard in a whisper. Because of my confusion, I almost pulled away when I heard Kate. She asked to be allowed to touch her butt? Ioni's thrill definitely made Kate question her earlier beliefs.

"Sure thing, babe," Matt replied. "I'll just use some oil to make it a nice massage."

Matt grabbed the oil and smeared it on Kate's ass. I could see him slowly rubbing the ball of his thumb around Kate's asshole. Suddenly I was torn back and forth what I was supposed to see, my cock spearing the sexy ass right in front of me, or my wife being fucked from behind while her asshole was being massaged by a very attractive man.

"How's that? Does that feel good?" Matt was very considerate and didn't want to scare Kate off.

"That's good. Really good. Please. Please keep doing that."

"Oh, God!! Shit! Keep it up. Fuck me!"

I wasn't sure who said that. Joni and Kate both seemed to be coming at the same time. I was numb myself, feeling so good with my dick deep up a tight, beautiful arse. Suddenly Joni's asshole started cramping on my dick. Her buzzing made her body shake. The pulse was in perfect timing with my thrusts. The grip of her asshole pulled the sperm right out of me and I sent several ropes deep into her ass.

At the same time I looked over to see Katie shaking as Matt pulled himself out. He sent his sperm all over her ass. He slowly and sensitively stroked his cock against her asshole as she came down from orgasm. My jealousy was washed away when I saw my wife, who looked so sexy, happy and wonton. Our sex life would change, so much is unknown, but I'm looking forward to it.

"Mmmm... I'm soooo tired..." Joni said as she collapsed on the couch. "I had originally planned to suck Matt's cock to sleep so I could get a taste of Kate, but he may have to wait until morning."

Kate twitched again, but I noticed that she didn't seem afraid of such a comment, as I had expected before that night.

"You have a shower in the guest bathroom next to the bedroom. I'm sure you want to clean up after our escapades. I know I'll want to take a hot bath. There are clean towels, and the sheets on the bed are fresh. Good night, you two. We had a wonderful evening."

"Thank you for your excellent hospitality. I'm exhausted, and I'm sure Kate feels the same way."

"Mmm hmmm..." murmured a naked Kate with heavy eyes.

"All right, off to the shower with you. Matt's sperm is still all over your ass." I said, as I helped her up on her feet and into the guest room. We entered the main hallway to the guest shower. Kate turned and held me as the warm water ran down our naked bodies.

"So... the night was... interesting."

"I gotta say. We're swingers now, my cock was in my colleague's ass, and you show up as a lewd bitch!"

Kate laughed at my generalization when she started soaping us both up. "What do you think about that? We've gone somewhere we've never been and we can't go back."

"I had a really hard time seeing you with Matt at first, but then I realized how sexy you looked, getting fucked like that in pure bliss. Since I'm usually the one fucking you, I hadn't seen you from that perspective. I was surprised when I realized how turned on I was. I mean, I was jealous when I saw some things, like you taking Matt in your mouth after he was inside you and making him play with your ass..."

While I was saying that, I casually dropped my hand on her ass and casually rubbed her crack up and down.

"How come I can't do these things?"

"Well, I was kind of caught up in that moment. A lot of things happened that I never thought I would do or agree with, but here we are. When I put Matt in my mouth, I didn't even think about how he'd been in my pussy, I just knew I wanted him to cum. Then I felt so sexy. It felt dirty, but empowering at the same time. And then when I saw how sexy you and Joni looked with your cock up her arse, I was jealous. Not that my husband was fucking another woman, but that she could enjoy anal sex so much. Made me wish I could do the same. I wanted to see if I could feel some of what Joni was feeling. Again, she felt dirty, but instead of feeling ashamed or disgusted as before, she felt dirty sexy. Somehow, I liked being that, what did you call me? A "wanton bitch"? Maybe we can try again sometime," Kate explained as she slowly soaped my cock. We had long since cleaned each other, but were still soaping each other up. I was hard again and wanted to make love to my wife. I slowly penetrated her with my finger and kissed her deeply. "Be gentle. I'm pretty tender from the pounding Matt gave me."

"We don't have to. We've both had a long night together and we don't have to overdo it."

"No! Please, don't... I need to feel you inside me. I need you to get inside my pussy! I just want you to be gentle. Please make love to me," Kate said as she started to pull my cock towards her opening. I put her back against the wall of the shower. I lifted her left leg so it was around her waist and slowly walked into her. We continued to kiss deeply while I gently stroked her in and out. As this position became a bit too much for Kate's back and leg muscles, I pulled her out and turned her around. She put her hands against the wall and spread her legs for me. As I entered her from behind, I turned her face backwards for another duel of our tongues. When I reached down and started stroking her clitoris, she immediately started to hum. Her pussy started to contract, which triggered my own orgasm. I pushed my cock as far as I could into her and got deep into her womb. It felt different than my previous orgasm tonight. It was amazingly sexy and pleasurable, but this one came from deep love.

We had been in the shower for over 30 minutes. I turned off the water and reached for the towels. I wrapped Kate in the fluffy white towel and kissed her again.

"I love you, honey."

"I love you, too, babe."

We slipped into the sheets and looked at each other. And we were both just laughing.

THE REUNION

Karyn rang the doorbell when she and Joe arrived at Walt and Jean's. It had actually been a year since the couples were together. From the inside, there was a muffled "Come in!" So the couple opened the door and went inside. Jean and Walt waited naked.

"It's so good to see you," Jean said excitedly. "I've been horny all week, just waiting for you to come!" She greeted Joe with a passionate kiss and began unbuttoning his shirt with one hand even before he closed the door. With the other, she felt his cock, which was growing fast in his pants, while Joe returned her greeting by bending down to suck her breasts. Walt did the same with Karyn, who was already walking up with her hands under her shirt and opening her bra.

Within a short time, Karyn and Joe were as naked as their hosts, their clothes scattered in random piles outside the front door, the four of them together with the spouses of the other side, who threw themselves directly into the activities of the weekend.

Jean and Joe lay on the floor. Walt let Karyn sit on the couch while he knelt between her legs. Jean and Joe eagerly explored each other's bodies, their hands clasped each other and familiarized themselves with the joys of their long-time sexual partners, who had been their first barter couple.

Jean happily felt Joe's cock as he sucked her breasts and rolled her nipples with his tongue. Their legs were intertwined, their bodies pressed together and rolled merrily on the floor.

"I missed your big cock so much!" Jean breathed hoarsely.

"He missed you too!" Joe replied, his cock was hard as a rock and throbbing as it felt its way between Jean's thighs. She felt it, reached out hungrily for him and began to caress him. Joe reached between Jean's legs and ran his fingers through her beautiful reddish-brown pubic hair. He found her swollen pussy lips and probed her inside with one finger, finding that she was wet and slippery.

On the couch Walt bent over and drilled with his tongue between Karyn's legs, which were spread wide to greet her. Jean and Joe looked over, just as Walt nibbled and Cudd on Karyn's labia, causing a purring excitement. He covered her pussy with his mouth, licked and sucked on her clitoris while she moaned with lust. She started rubbing her hips against Walt's face and then she clasped her hands behind his head and pulled him inside. She lifted her legs up on his shoulders and pulled him tight. Soon she rolled her head to the back of the couch and jerked her pussy hard against Walt's face, pressing his head between her strong thighs.

"Oh yeah, Walt," she called out. "I'm coming! Don't stop!"

Walt continued to whip over Karyn's clitoris until she spun and shook with her first orgasm of the weekend. When Karyn came down, Walt just kept going and pulled another climax, and then a third one until she finally straightened up and pushed Walt's face away from her pussy.

"Walt, that was fantastic!" she gasped. "Now it's your turn." She got up and they switched places. Walt's long dick pointed straight up at the ceiling, shaking with anticipation. Karyn bent over and kissed and sucked his cock head slightly and stroked his shaft with one hand while the other stroked his balls. She made happy humming noises in her throat and Walt just laid his head back and let the sensations of Karyn's mouth soak into his cock.

In the meantime, Jean and Joe had moved into a very nice, relaxed 69 position. Joe lay on the floor with Jean's pussy crunching on his face. She was lying on top sucking Joe's throbbing cock. Joe enjoyed the rich aroma of her vagina while she spread the thick juice of her arousal all over his face. Joe found it very sensual and arousing. The couple set a slow, leisurely pace for their intense oral explorations.

After a while, Joe and Jean noticed that things were starting to happen on the couch. While they paused to watch, Walt bucked his hips up off the couch, pressed his erection into Karyn's mouth, grunting and panting as she continued to suck on it.

"I will come," he told her, and she just nodded and hummed in agreement. "Oh yes", Walt moaned, and then, with a growl, he emptied his balls onto Karyn's face. Karyn eagerly extracted Walt's thick, milky-white sperm, applied every drop and then went back to collect the few drops that had escaped.

Jean and Joe enjoyed witnessing the mutual bliss of their spouses. It was incredibly hot to see Karyn carrying Walt's sperm on her face and tits and dripping it down. While she had blown Joe many times, it was somehow hotter to see her doing Walt.

Jean got up and moved to the other end of the couch, bending over her arm. "Come on, Joe," she urged, "take me from behind." Joe stood up, moved behind her and rubbed his cock against her wet pussy, annoyingly delaying her entry.

"Come on, Joe!" she shouted. "Fuck me! "Stick your big fat cock inside me and fuck me."

Not wanting to disappoint his friend, Joe pushed his hips forward and rammed the pulsating pole into her. Jean made a small gurgling sound in her throat as he pulled her almost completely out of her and rammed it back into her.

"Oh yes!" she shouted. "That's what I'm talking about!"

The couple settled into a steady rhythm. Joe bent over to fondle Jean's beautiful tits while they fucked. Joe enjoyed feeling the smooth, sweaty, damp skin of Jean's back against his chest. He loved to feel the beat of his balls against her clitoris at the end of each stroke. Soon, Jean gasped with the beginnings of her orgasm. As she reached her climax, she emitted a swaying moan, her cunt pressing Joe's rod as he slid further in and out of her. Eventually she shivered and trembled until the orgasm was complete. When he was sure she was done, Joe gave her one last forward push, palpated her to the core, then held on to her, his balls burst and sent a river of hot sperm into her before collapsing on the couch Karyn and Walt were watching.

Walt grinned as he listened to his wife struggling for breath. "This is how the weekend can begin," he giggled.

Everyone got dressed. Karyn and Joe took their bags to the guest room while Jean prepared a quick dinner. Then the friends went upstairs and piled into Walt and Jean's king-size bed.

After starting the weekend by mating across marriage lines, this time they mated with their own spouses. It was incredibly hot for Karyn and Joe to watch Walt and Jean make love, demonstrating their intimate knowledge of each other's bodies. While mating, Karyn and Joe made mental notes and even pointed out things to each other that Walt and Jean were doing and would try to do in the future.

Slowly and deliberately, Walt stroked Jean with his long tail while she purred and cooed with extreme pleasure as her husband's penis drilled into her deep. She wrapped her legs around his waist, then pushed them down his back, over his ass, and finally crossed her legs with his, fusing their bodies as she continued the waves of her horizontal mating dance.

Jean began to lift her hips from the bed and pressed against Walt's pushes, just as she had done with Joe before. He knew she would soon reach her climax. Her breathing was shredded and her hips snapped into her husband with increasing urgency. She began to moan to the rhythm of his thrusts, and soon Walt urged her: "Come with me, I want us to come together.

Walt began to roll his hips, aiming his spear at her core and grunting with every thrust, while Jean reached higher and higher plateaus of erotic pleasure. Finally, Walt growled, "Here it comes, babe!" and the two of them were lost in ecstasy as he sent his semen to his wife to mingle with Joe's earlier deposit.

Karyn and Joe watched as the mixture of Walt and Joe's sperm oozed out of her, around the shaft of Walt's cock, and slowly seeped into her ass. As they turned into position to watch, Karyn and Joe felt inspired by her example.

Karyn rolled Joe onto his back and began to slowly suck his cock, which pulsated with anticipation. She started with the balls and deliberately moistened every inch of his manhood sensually with her tongue, stopping at the tip to swirl her tongue around him a few times. This was all he could do to prevent him from getting right there and then.

With silky smooth movements Karyn glided along Joe's body, stopping to wrap her tits around his cock and give him a sultry titty fuck before continuing to glide seductively upwards until her breasts hung over Joe's mouth. Karyn moved from side to side, offering one breast first and then the other to suck while sliding her pussy back and forth along his upper body. As soon as her tits were satisfied, she slid back down and kissed Joe deeply. She slid further down until he could feel the tip of his cock pressing against her freshly shaved opening.

Karyn pushed further down until Joe's cock split her cunt lips, he could feel her warmth burning inside her. Slowly, Karyn continued until every inch of her favorite shaft was enveloped in the wet, sultry grip of her vagina until the base pressed against her pubic mound. Joe grabbed her ass cheeks and pulled them down, pressing the throbbing erection into her core.

As they had watched Walt and Jean, Karyn and Joe slowly fused their bodies until it seemed they were no longer two people but one. Joe's cock seemed to dissolve into the walls of his wife's pussy and every movement made every cell in their bodies tingle with erotic pleasure.

They mated slowly and sensually, for a long time, before the appreciative glances of their friends. Karyn and Joe put themselves on display for their friends and returned the former gift.

Joe held Karyn's body and enjoyed the feeling of feeling her naked skin against his own. Her breasts glided sensuously against Joe's chest, her nipples like little dots of erotic electricity that sent bumps through him. His hands caressed her thighs and ass cheeks and felt her muscles tense and relax with every thrust of her body. Finally, Karyn sat up and supported herself with her hands against Joe's chest. Her breathing became irregular and with each swing of her hips she became more determined and determined. She squeezed his cock with her muscles in her cunt, in time with her thrusts. In response, Joe began lifting his hips from the bed and urgently drove into her depths. Her fingers dug into his chest, and he gasped in pain after the little sting.

Then, with a soft howl, the dam broke from Karyn's climax. She twisted and writhed, trembling with the waves of orgasmic bliss that were crashing down on her. Her legs squeezed tightly around Joe's hips, and deep inside her a sob of lust surged forth. The sensations of Karyn's orgasm were as intense as anything Joe had ever experienced, so intense that he released into his own orgasm and joined her on a cosmic level of erotic bliss. Joe's body was riddled with orgasmic spasms and he felt as if the biggest charge of his life was shooting into her from his cock. He had virtually no control over his body. All he could do was let the orgasm run its course until it was complete.

When Karyn finally collapsed and struggled for breath, Jean spoke. "That was the most beautiful thing I have ever seen," she said.

"That's because you couldn't take care of yourself," Joe replied.

Then the four of them fell asleep happy and content.

In the morning, when the early sunrays were filtered through the blinds, Joe woke up dizzy and looked around. He and Jean were in the "middle" parts of the bed. Karyn lay on the edge next to Joe while Walt lay on the other side of Jean. During the night, Joe finally spooned with Jean, one hand cupping her breast. Joe thought it was a very pleasant way to wake up. He began to caress Jean's chest, squeezing it gently, stroking it, feeling its fullness and force. Joe's "morning glory" became even more pronounced and began to press into her ass crack.

Jean felt Joe's cock pressing against her ass and soon after, he came to Joe's attention. She turned her head to look over her shoulder. "Good morning, lover," she pulled reeling.

"Mmmmm. Good morning. Do you fancy a bit of morning fucking?" said Joe as he raised his hips to her ass and looked for a warm place to put his cock.

"Mmmmm. I'm always ready for a little morning fuck." She rolled her hips back to give the eager cock behind her better access to her pussy. She lifted her upper leg for a second and then reached between her legs to find the throbbing erection.

"Nice," she said to no one in particular. She led her friend's cock to her opening and pushed it into her. Then with the other hand, she pressed Joe's hand firmly against her chest while she slowly spooned. It was very relaxed, very gentle and unobtrusive.

After Jean and Joe had fucked for a while, Karyn turned around and got out of bed. She waded down the hall to the bathroom. When she came back, she went back to bed on Walt's side and started stroking his cock while she watched Jean and her husband fuck. When Walt woke up, Karyn rolled him on her back and started sucking his cock. She climbed on top of him, in the 69 position, Walt licked and played with her pussy while she sucked his cock.

Jean pushed Joe away briefly so that she could roll onto her back. She pulled him onto her, into a missionary position to resume the slow fuck. Slowly Joe pushed into her tight pussy, then pulled back until he had almost completely pulled out of her, then pushed back into her. She moaned as the thick cock spread her open and plunged in and out of her. When she began to hunch her hips, Joe reacted with even more violent blows until she whimpered with joy at her upcoming orgasm.

A few more punches and Joe began pumping sperm into her again as she writhed through another orgasm.

Jean and Joe turned around and watched as Karyn and Walt reached their destination. She was now seriously sucking his cock, stroking it with her hand and bouncing her head up and down along its length. She whirled her tongue furiously around the tip of Walt's tail, the pleasure was clearly written on

Walt's face. He made a small gurgling sound in his throat and put his hand on Karyn's back and tried to speak.

"Kar-," was all he could get before a sound came out of his throat somewhere between a grunt and moan, and he sent his semen back to Karyn's face and tits. Karyn made a happy purr when Walt came and continued to suck his cock until she had cleaned it thoroughly and his now soft cock slipped out between her lips.

Then she slipped backwards and presented her pussy to Walt's face. Walt gasped for breath for a few minutes, but this only had the effect of making him drink the rich, musky aroma of Karyn's cunt even deeper. When Walt had taken enough air, he drew back on Karyn's hips and put them on his face.

Karyn was happy to crunch her pussy on Walt's face and Walt in turn dipped into it with relish and made big slurping noises while licking and sucking his friend's wife. She moaned and groaned with relish as she rode on Walt's tongue and felt it enter her canal before finally settling on her clitoris. This caused Karyn to roll her hips at breakneck speed until she came with a trembling moan.

Walt might have thought his morning duties were over, but Karyn was not finished with him yet. As she lifted herself off his face, she turned around him and positioned herself on his tail. At first, she just spread him out by rubbing the crevices of her slit along the length of Walt's shaft to make it hard again. Jean and Joe smiled as they watched his cock expand. When she felt his hardness, Karyn lifted herself up for a moment and Walt's tail jumped up in readiness.

"I think he's ready," said Karyn and winked and smiled at her audience. "I can't believe it's Saturday morning and I haven't had that gorgeous long cock inside me yet. And with that she sat down again and slowly and deliberately impaled herself on Walt's stake.

Inch by inch, Walt's tail disappeared until she had swallowed it whole. She turned sensually on his shaft and purred with erotic pleasure to feel him penetrate deep into her as only he could. For several minutes she just sat still, pressing his shaft with her shells and enjoying the feeling of having penetrated to the furthest corners of her vagina.

Slowly she started rocking back and forth, rubbing herself sensually against Walt's long stick, moving it from one corner of her pussy to the other, moaning with erotic pleasure. Walt adapted to her slow rhythm, pushed his cock into her depths and then relaxed. Her spouses watched with fascination as they enjoyed her erotic dance.

Karyn moaned undaunted about the feelings that Walt's cock evoked in her. She steadily increased her speed until her ass was practically blurred as she pumped against his cock. Finally she came with a trembling moan that made Walt moan again when he shot his second load of the morning into her.

In the evening someone had the idea to put on some music and dance. Jean found a CD with dance music and we joined forces - Karyn danced with Walt and Jean danced with Joe. Of course all four of them were naked, it didn't take long before things started to move in an erotic direction.

When Joe danced with Jean, he felt increasingly aroused by the feeling of her naked body against his. He let one hand slide down from her waist to feel her bottom, stroking her cheeks, feeling her firm muscles as she moved and danced across the room. Jean snuggled up close to him, her left breast stomping against Joe's. He bent over and took her nipple in his mouth, rolled it on his tongue and enjoyed its taste and texture.

As Joe's cock hardened, Jean had a mischievous look on her face. She subtly tried to turn around to rub against Joe's throbbing erection. They stood face to face, bodies pressed tightly together, their breasts crushed Joe's chest, their hard nipples practically bored inwards. Joe grabbed her butt, one cheek in each hand, and she did the same. They kissed passionately, tongues intertwined, probing the corners of each other's mouths. Jean spread her legs slightly so that Joe's throbbing cock could rub against her pussy lips. Then they looked into each other's eyes, pulled each other tight and Joe's cock slid into them.

As soon as it was inside her, she pulled her legs together again, making her pussy feel even tighter. Of course, we really stopped dancing. But the standing fuck was even better. Normally her pussy was quite tight, but by pressing her legs together, it felt amazingly tight. Joe was pumping in and out of her. She was quite wet, but the friction from the increased tightness alone raised the sensations to an even higher level. Joe knew he wouldn't last much longer and as his climax approached, Joe sat down on the couch and Jean rode him. Soon it was grinding towards its own climax. When Joe knew she was coming, he raised his hips and sent another load of white-hot sperm into her.

While Jean and Joe recovered, he bent down to suck on her wonderful tits a little more while they watched their spouses. Walt left Karyn standing on a chair. She wrapped her arms around his neck while he hooked his elbows behind her knees to hold her up off the floor. He lowered her slowly until her opening met his cock. Then he slowly dropped her onto his cock, her whole weight pressing her down on him. Between Karyn's hands around Walt's neck and his arms that supported her knees, they could control her movements quite well. Joe watched in awe as they limped together vertically. It was obviously quite an athletic movement - Walt had to be strong enough to carry both their weight and still help Karyn to cope with the pressure of her own weight pressing on Walt's cock. And Karyn had to be strong enough to hold herself up with her arms.

They fucked like this for several minutes. When they got tired, Walt put Karyn on the couch and crawled between her legs to finish missionary style. Walt's long cock pumped in and out of

Karyn's sweet pussy until she breathed, "Come with me," and he sent his thick white cum back inside her.

Sunday was their last day together. They had formed a loose tradition that their last day together was the "day of three". They began by alternating the men with both women. Walt lay on his back while one of the women rode on his cock and the other one on his face. After each of the women had an orgasm in this position, they switched places until each came back. This time Walt Jean pumped the pussy full of semen when they were done.

At Joe's place both women sat next to each other on the couch while Joe licked their pussies. He loved to lean close to enjoy the smells and tastes of his two favorite vaginas. Jean was freshly filled with her husband's sperm, which contributed to the experience. As Karyn shivered through her second oral orgasm, Joe moved up and pushed his cock back into her, stomping furiously into her until she received another deposit of his hot sperm in her box.

Next it was Jean's turn to take on both men, she was dizzy with anticipation. Jean just loves it when two men take care of her pleasure at the same time. This time the boys "roasted her on a spit". Jean went in the "doggy position" on hands and knees, while Walt went on his knees in front of her and Joe went on his knees behind her. Jean sucked Walt's dick while Joe fucked her

from behind. At some point she practically threw Walt deep into her throat, with the thrusts from behind pushing her onto Walt's cock. The men managed to time it so that they let go almost simultaneously, with Joe's sperm squirting into her pussy and Walt's into her mouth.

When Walt and Joe had recovered enough from Jean to get a hard-on again, Walt sat down on the couch. Karyn reached for the bottle of lubricant and coated Walt's cock with plenty of lubricant. Then she sat down carefully and pressed her pussy against the tip of his cock. Slowly and gently she curled up on Walt's erection, stopping several times to adjust to Walt's length. As he sat well and safely with his cock in her cunt, she leaned back and invited Joe to lick her clitoris. Karyn moaned at the sensation of both types of stimulation. Walt started to slip and slide in and out a little faster while Joe tried to match Walt's movements with his tongue. Karyn writhed and writhed in front of the two sensations. She quickly reached her climax and she began to twitch, writhe and moan uncontrollably as the waves of lust rolled over her.

Walt and Joe just kept going, pulling orgasm after orgasm out of her one by one until she splashed on Walt's cock and Joe desperately tried to suck it all up until Karyn waved it off, spent. The boys stood over her and jerked off until they let their last load of this visit fly over Karyn's tits.

THE DIRTY WORK

It was the last class of the week, and so far my time had passed quite well. As a young and quite pretty substitute teacher I was used to badly disciplined school children with constant barbs about my shapely stupid blonde appearance. Dealing with the hooligan dynasty of alpha males and spiteful females trying to maintain their dominance was also a further prerequisite for survival. If nothing, then it considered me mean and harsh on the outside, even if I flinched on the inside. The jealous looks of the girls I taught, knowing that their friends wanted me more than they did, were also a constant in every class that I tried to control as much as I could. I was quite small and slightly overweight compared to the more marriageable cheerleaders in the class. Since I was only twenty-three years old, it seemed more like curvature than anything else. Unfortunately, despite my rather large bottom, I was quite flat-chested, and on those days when I was only filling in for other teachers, I didn't see any downside in filling out my bra to make me look stronger and more intimidating. I could handle teasing about my bottom, but since I was a teenager, I was very sensitive about my lack of cleavage. I must say that I cut an impressive figure with an accentuated bust, my light cream power suit and my red 4-inch heels. Even though I didn't always like some of the ruder comments that were often put in my way, if I'm honest, I knew I could have discouraged them with more.

Anyway, that Friday I found myself in a fairly upper middle-class high school in a mid-sized town in my home state of California. I had gone to high school there and was only a twenty-minute drive from my new apartment. It was my dream to find a permanent job here, and with my college debts growing exponentially, it was almost a necessity. Some of the staff remembered me from my time here as a rather uncouth favorite student, and certainly

Principal Harding appreciated me very much, although he might have preferred to remember me in my cheerleading outfit rather than my more elegant business suit. During the lunch break, I caught one of the older girls in my current class shitting the pants of a classmate and informed the principal. As a former victim of such pranks, I had no mercy for the perpetrator. I hoped that she would get into trouble and assumed that she would be given an immediate suspension so that I would not have to deal with her again as she had a rather scary appearance. So I was quite surprised to see her strolling into my last class and approaching me calmly, almost reluctantly.

"I am so sorry for the former Miss Gatting. It will never happen again. Please take this cup of coffee as a token of truce and no hard feelings. I know what I did was wrong and I hope that you can forgive me. Papa called me a terrible name..."

Papa? What did she mean by that? I was looking at my class list of names. I looked at my class list. The girl's name was Sylvia, Sylvia Harding, and she must be Principal Harding's daughter. Oh, God, how could I be so stupid as to think that that wouldn't have improved my chances of getting a permanent job or even a reference. So, in an effort to reconcile, I graciously accepted the cup of coffee, even though I neither drank coffee nor even liked it.

"Well, that's really a lovely gesture, Sylvia. I must say I was a little tired, so a cup of coffee should really cheer me up. Thank you, my dear, I hope you didn't go to too much trouble," I replied and tried to ingratiate myself with her.

When I took a sip of the coffee, I thought it tasted strange, but when she looked up at me excitedly, I looked down at her and nodded my appreciation. Within five minutes, thank God, I had drunk the whole cup and was able to get through my last lesson of the day comfortably. Everyone seemed to have behaved remarkably well so far, and I even began to relax a little and enjoy the lesson.

Then, about ten minutes after the class started, I felt a strange fullness in my stomach. As I stood at the blackboard trying to explain the relevance of the Canterbury tales to a disinterested bunch of teenagers, I suddenly felt a big pile up in my stomach. I stumbled briefly and could feel that the class noticed my discomfort. I tried to ignore it, but thirty seconds later the fullness gave way to a stronger cramping pain in my stomach. I felt the increase in pressure in my stomach and struggled to my stool to get a temporary respite. But it was no use. The pressure pushed down through my intestine and the cramps became almost unbearable. The urge to empty my bowels was insatiable. I knew immediately that something terrible would happen if I didn't get out of this classroom soon. I tried to stay as calm as possible, turned to the door and told the class that I would be back in a minute. I could feel their giggle and reuse as I stumbled, sweat building up on my forehead towards the door. I knew I didn't have much time as I turned the door handle before I was planning to flee madly down the hallway to the bathroom.

It no longer bothered me that over twenty-five pairs of eyes from eighteen-year-old students, all senior high school students, witnessed my embarrassing escape. But when I let the door come back towards me to open it, I realized that it would not move. For five desperate seconds I pushed and pulled desperately and without success, while the class became more and livelier as they watched my curious escapades. My need to defecate was overwhelming and as I looked back at the class, I could see that Sylvia was almost unimpressed by the madness of her classmates and the panic that emanated from me unabatedly. She was the only one who didn't seem

surprised by my irrational behavior. Another convulsive tremor flowed through my body, and only with intense physical will could I prevent the fatal faucal accident from happening. Finally, and with a devastating feeling of fear, I knew that I could not hold out much longer. I realized that someone had locked the door and asked for a key, but while the words were still leaving my mouth, another wave was seeping through my system.

"PLEASE, SOME HELP..." I cried out in horror as the reality of what was happening quickly dawned on me in class, when a horrible, elongated, flatulent event echoed from my rear end, drowning out even the loudest laughter in the class.

A vibrating fart bursting into decibels echoed wildly from my big ass. Only with my greatest willpower could I stop the fart before it changed from gaseous to semi-solid form. Nonetheless, this anal eruption made the class laugh, and it was clear that I would not get any sympathy from these teenage hyenas. Although it was only a fart, I knew I could not hold back the insidious forces that were holding my body hostage for much longer. Whatever was inside me was determined to leave, and with great reluctance I knew that the class would probably get a show they would never forget. Bizarrely, in the half seconds before the ultimate anal explosion, I resignedly debated in immense existential despair whether or not I would perform the nasty deed in my pants and make a massive mess of my clothes, or squat on the floor and empty myself on the floor. Neither, of course, was appealing. When I realized that I would have to leave the building later in some kind of clothes, I made the humiliating decision to quickly slip my suit trousers and panties over my ankles and squat in an inelegant manner in front of the class. This humiliating act brought the boys a primal spasm and the girls a hideous grin. Unfortunately, I didn't really hold my own down there. My blond bush was quite wild, and even in spite of the enormous situation I found myself in, there was still a clever Alec boy commenting on something ridiculous, which caused even more derisive laughter. So I squatted in my 4-inch heels, naked pussy and ass, which were displayed to over twenty children, and waited in disgust while a last, all-encompassing, throbbing and viscous wave of pain went through me until finally I could not stand it any longer. When I looked up, I noticed that by now all the kids had left their seats, and they followed my dirty demonstration in deepest excitement from all imaginable angles. They knew that they were witnessing something truly monumental.

When the resistance of my sphincter finally eased, I could feel an almost volcanic eruption shooting out of me. Some children from behind could actually see the poop lifting off my butt and starting its long fall to the floor, while others in front watched my trembling, sweaty face with tears falling down as I contorted mercilessly while aware of the exhibition I was offering. Only then did I see the multitude of telephone cameras, even a video camera, all of which caught me at an unflattering angle, and although I knew it was a terrible view, I did not want my naked image to be broadcast while I was performing this most evil of acts. So in a moment of madness I reached for my panties, and when the first elongated turd fell off my butt without further ado, I tore up my white cotton panties, caught the excrement in mid-flight and pulled them back up towards my still gushing butt. When it came in contact with my butt, it rubbed and squeezed itself around my now freshly covered butt. The smell was foul and the scene was relentless.

Unfortunately for me, the shit just kept coming back. Within seconds the panties filled up and almost unnaturally I felt that my now destroyed panties were full to the brim and the feces like riverbanks at high water flooded my panties in all directions. I was amazed at the sheer volume and speed of the action, for I am sure it was the bound schoolchildren.

The sinister look of disgust and ridicule continued when, after a short pause for breath, another massive surge of electricity came out of my anus. This time the discharge of excrement was so violent and explosive that even as I squatted there in my four-inch high heels, with my hands on either side of my cramped stomach, the sheer volume of faeces made my panties slide down my legs, leaving a brown, dirty trail. When they landed on my ankles, I knew immediately that they had destroyed my cream-colored pants, but that was the least of my worries at the moment.

The scene was unbearable. All these people stared in macabre fascination at their teacher, who humiliated herself in such a horrible way. Again, I saw the cameras pointed at my crotch and my bottom, which was now, of course, covered with an unbearable chocolate mess. The sheer volume was staggering, and finally it seemed as if the river, which had long been beyond my control, had come to a halt. My face begged for mercy, my mouth was incapable of speaking, while the bodies and cameras of my students around me pressed around their positions. The sound of flashes and giggles from the class continued until one boy held his camera almost directly under my crotch. I immediately clasped my hands to my stained pussy, hoping to fruitlessly fend off these photographic intruders. No sooner had I done that than I realized my mistake. The poop was frozen to my once blonde pubic hair, and when I touched it with my hands now, a big sticky mass ran onto my fingers. I looked down in horror, as if the events that were taking place were a nightmare, but as this was accompanied by further shockulence, I saw a camera in my face capturing my broken emotional state. Again, almost unconsciously I tried to shield my face as if the images had not already said a thousand words of humiliation. I put my hands in front of my face and as soon as I did so, my grave mistake became clear to me. The smell was obscene, but when I blocked my face with my hands, a volume of poop splashed over my once beautiful complexion. The make-up I had been wearing, already discolored by tears, was now drowning in the soft, sticky excrement from my intestines. Instead of protecting my face, I smothered it in my foul-smelling brew. More photos were taken and even more atavistic laughter was captured from the audience who, if they had once felt pity, were now completely immersed in my horrible ordeal. Still squatting, I tried to stand up, thinking my bowels could certainly not produce more, but when I bent my stomach to hear another original rumble from behind, it squeaked out. This time the contents were looser and gushed out painfully in one quick burst that lasted no longer than three seconds. But the effect was undeniable. A scatological spray formed like a puddle under my writhing body.

From the crowd of teenagers further collective cries of disgust were heard. The pain in my stomach began to subside and I looked down at my dirty panties, my legs and ankles, and the feelings of humiliation were overwhelming. I wanted to be somehow clean so that I could hide from the relentless looks. I rubbed my dirty hands off my sky-blue blouse to somehow free them from their impotence. Unfortunately, all I did was unknowingly leave another brown trace on my blouse. Everything I did was recorded, and every move I made was accompanied by the sound of "UGH!" and "GROSS!" or a variation of them.

In the midst of all this chaos, I once again encountered the bright light of Sylvia Harding, who seemed calmer than all the others, much like a peaceful lioness watching other lions tearing up scraps of meat. But in her eyes, I saw a serenity that I needed, and in my humiliating paralysis I felt that maybe she could offer me a break from this situation.

Almost instantly she jumped out of her chair and in an instant, she divided the crowd in front of me and looked down on me with something I felt was between pity and disgust.

"My goodness, what a mess you've made. Don't just stand there and admire your dirty work, why don't you at least try to cover your dirty vagina with the suit jacket?

I still felt paralyzed, but amazingly the girl stepped behind me and almost involuntarily she slid the shoulders of my suit jacket over my flaccid arms and back. In one quick movement she wrapped the suit jacket around the front of my upper body. She was right; at least my front was covered, even though my bottom was still completely exposed. Maybe she was trying to help.

"Now do exactly as I say and this nightmare will soon be over," she whispered to me.

I obeyed as in hypnosis. Suddenly the laughter of the crowd in my head stopped and for a while I only heard the voice of Sylvia who helped me out of my crisis. I nodded submissively and when she ordered me to take off my blouse, since I had destroyed it with my dirty hands, I couldn't help but obey her. Slowly I opened the blouse and wiped even more shit from my hands while pressing the buttons. Finally I had taken off the blouse and looked at Sylvia for further instructions. She told me to throw it in the corner of the room and as I did so I heard another collective "OOH!

Now only dressed in a bra and with a jacket wrapped around her crotch, I looked at Sylvia for further instructions.

"Oh my God! Is your bra padded or what? I'm sure I can see that there's paper hidden in your bra," she asked almost rhetorically.

I was too stunned to answer, I just looked down and could only slightly see the paper loop hanging loosely from my ruffled oversized bra, but I couldn't believe that in the midst of all the other hustle and bustle she would have noticed it so quickly. My stunned expression and my guilty behavior were answer enough for Sylvia.

"You're lucky you have something to wipe your dirty ass with MsSCATing," Sylvia announced as she dug her hands into my bra and like a magician pulled paper out of one sleeve and unfolded the huge rolls of paper until my bra hung listlessly and loosely from my body.

I wondered if she was calling me Miss Scating for a moment as I complied with her request.

When she handed me the bundled toilet paper that gave me confidence, she ordered me to clean myself.

I knew that what I was doing was ridiculous, but I was still trapped in the room, and since I had no other options, I just stuck to the one person who seemed to have authority. Still on my heels, the lower half of my body covered with poop, my face grazed too much, as if I had just had a poop facial, but my upper body only with traces. My white bra and my white body offered a strong contrast to all this. I crouched down to wipe my bottom and as I did so, the suit jacket slipped off and revealed my smudged front again. Once again exposed I tried to follow Sylvia's orders when she told me to ignore my nakedness. Unfortunately, despite the toilet paper I didn't make much progress in the mess I had made. I tipped the dirty cloth on the floor in the stinking puddle of excrement where I was standing.

As a variety of thoughts flashed through my mind, including how I might ever get home or even get clean or get over this incident, I felt Sylvia unhook my bra in the back... "You're still dirty...need something else to clean yourself...hmmm, how about this thing, it doesn't seem to work anymore.

Crazy, despite all I had been through, I still felt humiliated because of my not very luscious breasts. On another day it would have been a shattering experience if I had been discovered that I had falsified my appearance as I had been. It shouldn't have mattered in connection with the last fifteen minutes, but when I submissively started to remove my bra from my body, I wished the bottom could have opened up and swallowed me right there. Instead, more people than ever before got an unencumbered view of my naked breasts as in the midst of a fresh round of quick-tempered and angry laughter and the dots, glances and flashing cameras I tried to use my bra to wipe my dirty bare bottom clean.

In each cup I scooped a large amount of the sticky, smelly substance. My hands were now completely brown, as the excess was matting on my skin. I couldn't believe that I had wiped my butt completely naked in a classroom full of students after I had performed the most private of all actions right in front of their eyes.

"OH MY GOD, THIS IS THE MOST REVOLVING THING I EVER SEE", exclaimed just one of the many voices that penetrated the crowd.

"AND OH MY GOD, LOOK AT HER TINY TITS. I CAN'T BELIEVE I THOUGHT I THAT THAT BITCH WHAT HOT!', cried another voice.

How humiliating and for some reason the barbs on my tiny breasts still hurt deeply. Maybe I should cover them, I thought to myself, and almost in post-traumatic shock I tried to adapt the dirty bra back to my body. Immediately I felt the poop being squeezed against my breasts and dripping into my stomach. Sylvia looked at me with dismay.

"This is just disgusting, if you want to leave this classroom, I suggest you take this oversized bra made of poop off your body. I mean really, just look at the mess you've made of your clean and perverted little bosom. It seems to me that you must have a scat fetish or something," said Sylvia, leaving me little choice but to take the bra off again and let it fall to the floor so that now a boob covered with steaming poop appears.

"Luckily, my dad gave me the key to school, so why don't I escort you to the locker room and you can borrow this... "and you can wash that dirt off the body. I mean, oh my God, look at you, you're fucking disgusting now, right? Now take off your dirty panties and pants and we can take care of it!"

I couldn't help feeling the disgusting taste when I wiped them with my hands so dirty. She was right, I was disgusting, but when my mind gained temporary clarity, I thought why the door was locked, why, if she had a key, she didn't try to open the door earlier.

"Stop hesitating and take it off at once," she moved again and threw those thoughts out of her head again.

Anyway, the task wasn't so easy in four-inch heels and standing in a puddle of excrement. I knew I had to take off my heels to get the job done, but I didn't want to stand barefoot in my own mess, so I was hoping briefly to be able to take the dirty clothes off my feet while I was still wearing my heels. So, I stood my left foot on half the clothes and quickly raised my right foot to do the job. This turned out to be even harder than I imagined, and as I jumped from foot to foot trying to take off the dirty clothes, I saw my whole body vibrate wildly. If I had big breasts, I would know they would be swaying madly now, but when I suddenly released the left side of my panties and pants from my left heel, a new swing made me lose balance with my right and slipped, as if on ice, first face the pelvis below. The consistency of this looser, more liquid pile was quickly washed all over my body when I hit the ground, practically swimming. The front of my body was now completely covered with various shades of brown, including the face, and while I was soaking in the search for air, I tossed my body on my back to open my mouth to the air. Lying there in what was now a complete humiliation, I looked up at Sylvia, who was rising above me. She was now laughing mercilessly at me and I saw evil in her eyes. And then he hit me almost like a stone between my eyes, as bright as day. Coffee, keys...

ghtning Source UK Ltd.
on Keynes UK
W051043260521
UK00020B/336